# MICROSAURS

## TINY-TRICERA TROUBLES

# MICROSAURS

## TINY-TRICERA TROUBLES

## DUSTIN HANSEN

Feiwel and Friends
New York

A FEIWEL AND FRIENDS BOOK
An imprint of Macmillan Publishing Group, LLC
120 Broadway, New York, NY 10271

Our books may be purchased in bulk for promotional, educational,
or business use. Please contact your local bookseller or the Macmillan Corporate
and Premium Sales Department at (800) 221-7945 ext. 5442 or by email at
MacmillanSpecialMarkets@macmillan.com.

Library of Congress Control Number: 2018955575
ISBN 978-1-250-09038-6 (hardcover) / ISBN 978-1-250-09040-9 (ebook)

Book design by Liz Dresner
Feiwel and Friends logo designed by Filomena Tuosto
First edition, 2019

10  9  8  7  6  5  4  3  2  1

mackids.com

*For Kathleen, my costume maker,*
*my creative mentor, my hero.*
*But most of all, my mom.*

# CHAPTER 1
## THE 48TH ANNUAL GREAT TOMATO FESTIVAL

"What if you don't like tomatoes? I mean, it's not like this is the great cotton candy festival. Everyone likes cotton candy. I bet half the people on the planet don't even like tomatoes," Lin said as we made our way through the crowd.

"Everyone in this town likes tomatoes," I said.

"That's not true. That can't possibly be true because I don't like tomatoes," Lin said as she took a flyer from a guy wearing a red jacket. "Thanks," she said with a smile. I noticed her teeth were kind of pinkish.

"Maybe not fresh, raw tomatoes, but even you like tomato candy," I said.

"I'd eat dog food candy if there were such a thing." Lin stopped in the middle of the crowd. "Wait. I just had an idea. We should make candy for dogs. We'd be RICH!"

I was thinking that Lin might be onto something, when I heard the *blip* sound in my ear that told me someone had just turned on

their SpyZoom Invisible Communicator. I could tell by the expression on Lin's face that hers had just blipped, too.

"Hey, Vicky. Is that you?" I asked. To the people standing around us it looked like I was talking to myself, but I didn't care. I knew better.

"Yeah. Where are you guys?" Vicky chirped in our ears.

"We're by the tomato juice dunking booth," Lin said. "And look at that. They are looking for volunteers."

"Ha ha. Very funny, Lin. You're not going to talk me into that today. I'm the Grand Marshal for the Tomato Parade. I got my hair done, I'm wearing a brand-new outfit, and I'm going to be on stage in, like, three minutes. Which brings me to my first question. Where are you guys and why aren't you HERE WITH ME?" Vicky said without taking a breath.

"We're on our way. It's just really busy out here. We'll be there soon," I said.

"Do you have your tickets?" Vicky asked.

"Yup. Your mom's assistant dropped them off at my house this morning. Thanks, Vicky," Lin said, then rolled her eyes. The Invisible

Communicators are pretty awesome, but they aren't sensitive enough to pick up eye rolls.

"See you soon, Vicky. Have fun today," I said, then tapped my earbud, turning off the communicator. "Come on. We gotta run."

Lin and I darted through the crowd outside the big stadium in the center of town. The famous Ramp-O-Saurus, the largest skateboard jump in the world, towered above everything, casting its long-necked shadow down on the festival. The line at the stadium was pretty big, but we had special guest tickets, so we got right in. A nice man wearing a tomato hat, a Ruby Girls concert T-shirt, and thick-rimmed glasses took us to our seats, then gave us each a towel covered in red, purple, and pink sequins.

"What are these for?" Lin shouted at the usher.

"You're in the splash zone. The Grand Marshal

is going to smash the opening ceremony tomato. You'll be glad you had the towel, believe me," he yelled back with a smile. "Enjoy the concert."

Music pumped through speakers as big as a semitruck, and the crowd was singing along, dancing, and shouting so loud I could barely hear myself think. I leaned over to Lin, holding the sparkling towel in my hands. "This isn't going to dry anything. It's covered in glitter," I shouted.

"I guess you can use it like a shield." Lin was holding the tiny towel in front of her face. "Or you could stuff it in your ears so you don't have to hear the concert."

"I think you'd need more than a towel to do that. Maybe some tomato-flavored bubble gum," I yelled.

"Why are we here anyway? I can't stand the Ruby Girls," Lin screamed.

"We're not here for the music," I shouted as
hundreds of brightly colored laser lights began
to flicker on the stage. The crowd went wild,

shouting and jumping up and down so loud that the stadium began to rock. I'd be lying if I said it wasn't exciting. Okay, I'm not what you'd call a Ruby Girls groupie, but I've heard their music and it's hard not to want to dance along when there is so much energy bouncing around at a live concert. A booming voice rumbled through the massive speakers. "Ladies and gentlemen. Tomato lovers around the world. Welcome to the Forty-eighth Annual Great Tomato Festival."

The mob of tomato fans went bonkers, and the voice continued. "As you know, one lucky person is elected as the Grand Marshal of the Tomato Parade, but that isn't the end of their duties. That lucky person also gets to kick off the concert by smashing the ceremonial first tomato!"

More cheering and roaring by the thousands of excited people surrounding me. Lin and I had been let in on the secret, but the rest of them had no idea who this year's Grand Marshal was, and they were cheering for the announcement.

The crowd only grew louder as a platform, covered in tiny, shining mirrors that bounced rainbow-colored reflections all around, lowered from the ceiling. Our newest adventure partner was facing away from the crowd, holding a huge mallet over her shoulder.

"Time to meet our Grand Marshal. Join us in welcoming Victoria Van-Varbles," the announcer said, and everyone went nutso. I looked over at Lin and even she was yelling and shouting for Vicky.

Two ushers wearing the tomato hats came on stage. One was carrying a sturdy-looking stool, and the other was packing the biggest tomato I had ever seen in my life. Vicky turned around on the platform and her new, replacement limited-edition Ruby Girls tour jacket sparkled almost as much as her wide smile. She held the hammer over her head and the crowd lost their minds.

"Hey there, tomato fans! It's me, Victoria! Are you ready to get this party started?" Vicky said, and her voice echoed off the back wall of the stadium. The people erupted, and Vicky did a little dance with the hammer.

"Are you ready for the best band on planet

Earth? RUBY GIRLS!" Vicky said, and I thought the stadium was going to split in two it was so loud.

"Well, before they can come out, there's something I need to do," Vicky said. She put the head of the huge hammer on the ground and leaned against the handle. She scratched her head and pretended to be thinking really hard, but the crowd knew.

"SMASH IT! SMASH IT! SMASH IT!" they chanted, and I couldn't help it. I chanted along with them.

"Oh. That's right. I need to smash this little, tiny tomato with my itsy-bitsy hammer," Vicky said. She swung it around as she approached the tomato, which was waiting to be pummeled on the sturdy stool in the center of the stage. Lin and I were sitting so close I could honestly smell the tomato, and as Vicky pulled the hammer behind her head, I noticed the first three rows lift their sequined towels over their faces. But I didn't. I wanted to watch it sploosh. I'd had worse things than tomato guts on me before. Much worse.

Vicky brought the hammer down with a THUD! It was a direct hit! Tomato seeds, juice,

and pulpy-fleshy red chunks flew through the air.

It was pure pandemonium. All the rainbow-colored lights turned red and the music thumped faster and faster. Everyone around me was jumping and dancing as the chant changed to "Vicky! Vicky! Vicky!"

I was joining in the fun when I felt something buzz in my pocket. I pulled out my phone and saw that I was getting a video call from Professor Penrod. I showed it to Lin. She held up a finger to tell Professor Penrod to wait one second, and started pulling me out of my seat.

Vicky announced the Ruby Girls, then ran off stage as Lin and I made our way out of the wild, out-of-control crowd. The hallway surrounding the stadium was still loud and I could feel the beat rumbling beneath my feet, but at least I could hear myself think.

I held the phone up to get another look at Penrod and saw that he and Carlyle were obviously inside the Microterium. I could tell because Bruno was scratching his collar with his back foot in the background.

"Hey, Professor. Hello, Dr. Carlyle. How are you two?" I asked as Lin peeked over my shoulder and waved.

"Oh, hello you two. Are you safe? It looked like you were inside a volcano," Penrod said with a concerned look on his dirty face.

I nodded, and Lin answered, "You saved us from something worse. We were about to be stuck inside a Ruby Girls concert."

"Oh. By all means go back, then. Have fun. What I need can wait," Professor Penrod said.

"Are you sure, Penny?" Dr. Carlyle asked.

"Yeah. Are you sure, Penny? Because we're just waiting for an excuse to leave this place," Lin said.

"Well, we are in a bit of a bind here in the Microterium," the professor said.

"Not the first time I've heard that sentence," I said, but even as I said it I was looking forward to helping out. It had been a long, VERY long week since we'd been back to the Microterium. Dr. Carlyle and Professor Penrod were making some big changes to try to make the place safer and healthier for the Microsaurs. Professor Penrod said what they were doing was pretty risky because he was rebuilding the shrink and expand devices from scratch, and the chance of getting stuck tiny for the rest of our lives was too much to ask of us. Lin and I did not agree, but we obeyed.

"True. What do you need?" Lin asked, as eager as I was.

"Well, we could use some food supplies. A little lunch would be nice. But most important, we need someone to stop by and test the new Expand-O-Shrink-O-Portal," Professor Penrod said with a proud smile on his face.

"It's done?" I asked, feeling that nervous excitement I always feel when I know adventure is nearby.

"It sure is. We were wondering if you two would like to run down with some snacks and join us for a picnic in the Microterium," Dr. Carlyle said.

Lin didn't even wait to reply. She started running full tilt out of the stadium.

"I'll take that as a yes," Professor Penrod said.

"You bet. We'll be there in fifteen minutes max. I hope you like carnival food," I said as I waved good-bye, then chased after Lin.

# CHAPTER 2
## BACK IN THE MICROTERIUM

On our way out of the festival we picked up some of the most popular snacks for our Microterium picnic: fried green tomato slices, cheese pizza slices with extra marinara sauce, and my favorite—bright red and super-delicious sun-dried-tomato-crusted corn dogs. Lin bought some strawberry-tomato soda; tomato brownies,

which I was not so sure I wanted to try; and just
before we zipped off to Penrod's, she bought
her favorite tomato lollipop and tucked it in her
back pocket. By the time we made it out of the
park there was nobody around. Pretty much the

entire town was inside the stadium, rocking out with Vicky and the Ruby Girls.

We hurried to Professor Penrod's place, ran through his backyard, and let ourselves into his secret barn-lab.

"Well, that was fast," Professor Penrod said as he stood up from the lab stool. He was working on some complicated wiring fixed to a blue switch. I wanted to know what it was the second I saw it, but before I could ask, Dr. Carlyle spoke.

"And whatever you brought along for lunch smells delicious," she said. She held out her arms and gave Lin a big hug. "It's nice to see you again, Lin."

"Nice to see you, too, Dr. Carlyle," she said. "I hope you're hungry."

"I'm starving," Dr. Carlyle said. "I almost started eating the Microbites."

"You should. They're pretty good," Lin said with a grin, and Dr. Carlyle laughed.

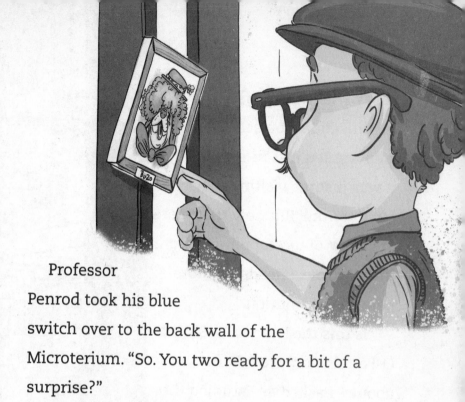

Professor
Penrod took his blue
switch over to the back wall of the
Microterium. "So. You two ready for a bit of a
surprise?"

"Always," Lin said, and I nodded along.

Professor Penrod twisted the framed picture
of his prized dog, Bruno, and the back wall of the
barn-lab lowered into the floor. I looked out into
the Microterium and was shocked. It looked so
lush and green inside. Far more dense than it had
in the past. But that wasn't all that had changed.

"Where's the big metal step?" Lin asked.

"Very observant, young Lin," the professor

said. "That was my first modification. You see, the metal step worked just fine when it was just me visiting the Microterium. But now that there are a few of us stopping by from time to time, I needed a more permanent solution."

"Is this the Expand-O-Shrink-O-Portal you were talking about?" I asked as I studied the new contraption.

"Positively perceptive, Danny. It is one and the same," Professor Penrod said.

Instead of using the big metal step as a trigger to turn on the old Shrink-A-Fier, there was now a shiny aluminum frame, like a big doorway between the

barn-lab and the Microterium. I looked around for the massive showerhead and the coils and coils of clear plastic tubing, but I couldn't see any of it.

"Where's the rest of it?" I asked.

"It's imbedded inside the metal frame itself. This is my finest invention, Danny old boy. You see, not only will the portal shrink you down to size, but if you look carefully down below, you'll see a matching portal about the size of a thumbtack inside the Microterium. I've rigged the Shrink-A-Fier and the Expand-O-Matic into one single invention. And all you need to do is flick this blue switch to turn it on and walk through the portal. Then blam-o-shrink-o, you'll be small. Reverse the process on the other side, and zap-o-expand-o, you'll be right back here at normal size," he explained.

"Excellent," I said, totally impressed.

"And you moved the Fruity Stars Lab 3.0,"

Lin said as she crouched down to look into the Microterium. Directly below the entrance, the plastic PIBBs building waited in the lush jungle that surrounded it. Right where the old copper penny used to sit I saw a tiny square frame of aluminum.

"Absolutely," Dr. Carlyle said. "We needed to move it closer to the entrance. I know nobody planned on this, but walking from the step to the old location of the Fruity Stars Lab caused quite a bit of environmental damage. Big feet plus small plants, well, that's not a good combination. This way, after you get the hang of it, you can take a step up into the barn-lab while you expand, and you'll be right back where you started without putting a massive toe in the Microterium."

"That sounds awesome," Lin said. She turned to Professor Penrod. "When do we get to try it?"

Professor Penrod flicked the switch to turn

on the Expand-O-Shrink-O-Portal. I could hear the orange shrinking liquid start to bubble in tubes hidden inside the aluminum frame. A small motor began to whir and a faint, orange-smelling mist puffed inside the frame.

"Well, I promised you a picnic in the Microterium. Now seems like a good time," Professor Penrod said.

"So we just step through? That's all?" I asked, but Lin wasn't waiting for an answer.

"See ya soon, baboon," she said as she jumped through the Expand-O-Shrink-O-Portal. She seemed to disappear right before my eyes, but I knew she was ant-sized and happy inside the Microterium.

"I guess that's my answer," I said.

Professor Penrod motioned to the framed opening. "After you, Danny."

"You don't need to ask me twice," I said as I stepped through.

The orange mist that surrounded me felt cool against my summer-toasted skin. The familiar dizzying feeling returned, and as I began to shrink I took a step toward the Fruity Stars Lab 3.0. In a jiffy I was standing in the Microterium with Lin.

I heard something swooshing toward us and watched as Dr. Carlyle and Professor Penrod shrank down at the same time. They joined us with wide smiles on their faces.

"That was AMAZING!" I said. "Wow. So much easier."

"Yeah, but I'm going to miss the Slide-A-Riffic," Lin said.

"Oh, that reminds me. I've relocated your gondola-like contraption, and it has been so handy I was wondering if you could build us a few more," Professor Penrod said.

"More what? Slide-A-Riffics?" I asked.

"Yes. I think if we had five or six more we could station them along the railway. They could be drop-off points that we could use to move quickly through the Microterium," Professor Penrod said.

"A railway station?" Lin asked.

"Oh my goodness. We have so much to catch you up on. Yes. We've added a train to the Microterium. We have to take a ride later, but first, it's picnic time," Professor Penrod said.

"You can say that again," Lin said, so of course, Penrod did.

Lin and I unpacked the lunch. We placed the greasy, delicious-smelling, super-tomatoey items on the dice we like to use as a table. The smell attracted a few visitors, as it always does in the Microterium, and before long Pizza and Cornelia were chasing Bruno around as they playfully waited for their own picnic.

"Just wait until you see what Dr. Carlyle has done to Frank's Bog. It's now a fantastic fungi forest fit for a king," Professor Penrod said. He flicked the switch on his new invention to make sure it was all working correctly, then joined us at the dice.

"These corn dogs are amazing," Dr. Carlyle said. "It's like they come with their own ketchup."

"I know, right?" Lin said with her mouth full.

Behind us, Pizza and Cornelia romped and
played with Bruno as we munched our lunch.
I had just taken a big bite of corn dog when I
watched Bruno trip backward over a log. This

would normally be something Bruno would
actually enjoy, and certainly something that
would make us laugh, but this time his trip
sent him in the worst possible direction.

Directly through the Expand-O-Shrink-O-Portal. Next thing I knew, I was looking up at a large puppy-saurus. In less than a second, Bruno had expanded. From my ant-sized point of view, he looked larger than a skyscraper.

"WHAT? That's impossible!" Professor Penrod shouted as he jumped up from his seat, but it was too late.

"How did that happen?" I asked. It made no sense. Things were only supposed to go back to "normal" size. Bruno had grown to the normal size of his ancestors, turning him from Microsaur to dinosaur in a blink of an eye.

"Is the portal still on?" Lin asked, looking as confused as I felt.

"I didn't think so, but accidents happen," Professor Penrod said.

"Quick. Turn it off!" Dr. Carlyle shouted, but once again it was too late. Pizza and Cornelia chased after the rolling Bruno, dashing through the portal and exploding into giants. Their shadows covered most of the Microterium, and filled my heart with panic.

The sound of the barn-lab being tossed around rattled loud in our ears, and the four of us went immediately into rescue mode.

"We'll stay here and figure out what happened to the Expand-O-Shrink-O-Portal. You two go get the Microsaurs before, well, before it turns into a disaster!" Professor Penrod shouted as we jumped into action.

"Let's go!" Lin yelled, and I started running alongside her. We dove through the portal and landed inside the barn, back to regular size. Boxes had been knocked from the shelves, and there was a large hole in the front door of the barn-lab.

Lin was a few steps ahead of me, and she looked out the hole in the door. "Oh my gosh. They are massive," she whispered.

I walked up behind her and saw them. Bruno was rolling on his back in the grass, and Pizza was watching Cornelia bonk her head against an apple tree. Little green apples were falling down around them like unripe hail. Something about seeing them in the real world really did make them look much bigger, but there they were. Three large, young Microsaurs, looking more dinosaurish than ever before.

"What do we do?" Lin said.

"Same thing we do in the Microterium, I guess. Go hang out with them and try to get them to walk back through the portal," I said.

"All right. You go get Bruno, and I'll pick some of those apples and try to use them to tempt the twins. It looks like they are enjoying them."

Lin went off toward the old apple tree, and I quietly walked toward my trusty pal. "Hey, Bruno. Wanna give me a ride, big guy?" I asked.

Bruno stood up, looked over at me, lolled

his big pink tongue out of his mouth, and panted.

"That's a good boy," I said as I approached.

"Now come, buddy. Let's get you back to the Microterium."

I looked over at Lin. She was trying to

convince Cornelia to stop thumping the apple tree, and Pizza was finding the whole thing hilarious. I was about to run and jump on Bruno's back when I heard loud music thumping in the air. The music caught Bruno's attention, too. I wasn't sure if he'd ever heard music before, but he immediately liked it. He started bounding from right to left, and he shook his head. If we were in the Microterium, it'd be downright adorable, but something about the way he was acting made me nervous. If he decided the music was something worth chasing, there wasn't much I could do to hold him back.

The music was getting louder as Bruno began dancing his way to the front of Professor Penrod's house.

"Hang on, buddy. You're going the wrong way," I said.

Then the worst thing I could have ever

imagined happened. The source of the music drove around the corner, right into Bruno's view. It was the Tomato-Mobile in all its shiny red glory.

Bruno lowered his head and charged as the music-playing Tomato-Mobile zoomed away, heading toward the festival. The fence that surrounded Professor Penrod's yard crumpled like paper as Bruno smashed through it, heading for trouble.

# CHAPTER 3
## COME BACK!

"Lin!" I shouted, but she had already seen what had happened.

"Pizza. Cornelia. You stay!" she said in her stern, dog-trainer voice. Pizza sat and Cornelia rolled over. Not exactly what she had in mind, but close.

I ran through the truck-sized hole Bruno had

burst in the fence, and before long I could hear Lin's skateboard rolling up behind me. I couldn't see Bruno, but it was easy to tell where he had been. A stop sign was bent in half, a bed of red roses was smashed to smithereens, and a red wagon had a big Bruno nose horn–sized hole right in the middle of it.

"What are we going to do?" Lin asked as she caught up to me.

"I have no idea," I admitted as I jumped over a red bicycle in the sidewalk that was twisted up like a pile of spaghetti. I heard big footsteps and turned to look. Pizza and Cornelia were running up behind us, and I nearly screamed in frustration. We needed fewer Microsaurs running around, not more. Lin saw them, too, and skidded to a halt.

"What are you doing?" I asked.

"We need help," she said as she held out her hands and stopped the twins. "And these two are going to give it to us."

"But . . . what can they do?" I asked.

"If these two Microsaurs can round up a whole herd of stampeding stegos, they can certainly help us catch Bruno," she said. She took a step on Cornelia's large back leg, then climbed on her back. Cornelia looked shocked at first, then roared so loud it gave me the shivers. I looked over at Lin. She wasn't worried a bit. In fact, she was grinning from ear to ear, which made me feel a bit more confident.

"But I have never ridden a T. rex," I said, looking into Pizza's big round eyes.

"Neither have I," Lin said. "HeYA!" Lin nudged Cornelia's ribs with her heels and they were off, following Bruno's path of destruction.

"All right, Pizza. Let's do this." I carefully climbed aboard the towering T. rex, and he took off after his sister. After riding Bruno, riding Pizza was like riding a rocket ship covered in muscles and scaly skin.

On the one hand, I guess we were lucky to have the tomato festival going on the same day that three dinosaurs were running through town. On any other day, we'd have been spotted immediately. Riding two dinosaurs down the street would have been the biggest news story of the century. Heck, of the last 64.5 million years, ever since they went extinct. But on the other hand, we couldn't have picked a worse day for Bruno to find his way to our regular-sized

world. There was something about the color red that drove the normally lovable and super-obedient Microsaur totally wacko.

We entered the parking lot that surrounded the festival to the sound of car alarms ringing in the air. The alarms were only coming from red cars, so at least we knew we were heading in the right direction.

"I'm not getting a good feeling about this," I said to Lin as we rode toward the stadium on the backs of two very obvious Microsaurus rexes.

"Yeah. Me neither. And I have some bad news," she said, pointing straight ahead as she pulled Cornelia to a stop. "It looks like Bruno found the Tomato-Mobile." Sure enough, there was the big tomato-shaped truck lying on its side near the entrance of the festival grounds.

"Great. Just what we need," I said.

Then Lin and I rode the twins toward the smashed Tomato-Mobile.

# CHAPTER 4
## THE TOMATO-MOBILE

"Oh man, this is bad," I said. The Tomato-Mobile was toppled, its wheels still spinning in the air.

"Really bad," Lin agreed.

The back door to the Tomato-Mobile was swinging wide open, so we peeked inside. "Hey. Is there anybody in here?" I asked, but it was pretty obvious that the driver had run away. Probably terrified out of their mind.

Lin pushed her way past me and entered the tomato truck. "There are three Bruno-horn-shaped holes in the side of this thing. I can see the sky through them."

"Are you serious? He actually punctured the Tomato-Mobile?" I said, half worried and half impressed.

Cornelia followed Lin through the back door of the truck and entered the tomato. I could hear Lin giggling as she tried to make room for her oversized friend.

"Hey, Lin. Is there room for two T. rexes in there?" I asked in a hurry.

"Uh, maybe, but it'll be tight," she said. "Why?"

"Because we have company. Scoot over," I said. I pushed Pizza toward the door and he happily smashed inside with his sister. Since the two Microsaurs shared a single egg, they loved smashing into tight spaces together.

Lin climbed out the front door of the truck, coming out on top.

"Quick. Jump down. They're coming!" I said.

"Who's coming?" Lin asked.

I pointed across the parking lot at the two people who were obviously heading in our direction.

"Oh man, I'm going to say it again," Lin said.

"Yeah. Me too," I said.

Then we both spoke together at the same time. "This is bad."

We were standing with our backs to the door of the Tomato-Mobile, and just before our two visitors got to us, I noticed the top of a Microsaurus rex tail sticking out the door. I stuffed it inside. "You two be nice and quiet. Okay?" I said, just before I closed the door.

"It was right here. I'm not kidding," a man wearing a puffy tomato hat and a bright red shirt said. "It was a real rhinoceros. I mean, it had to be. What else could knock over my precious Tomato-Mobile like this?"

He was frantic, but the security guard he had with him was as calm as could be. She looked around at the truck, then at the two of us. She looked like one of those gruff detectives on TV, and I had a feeling she was going to get to the bottom of the upturned Tomato-Mobile filled with Microsaurs in about thirty seconds. She studied Lin and me up and down, then turned back to the driver.

"So, Mark. What you're telling me is that a rhino chased you through town, smashed into every red car in this parking lot, then rammed into the side of your precious tomato truck," she said.

"Tomato-Mobile," Mark, the driver, corrected.

"Yes. The rhinoceros rammed into the side of your Tomato-Mobile, flipping it over in the parking lot," she said. She pulled out a little notebook and wrote down a note.

"Exactly. That's exactly what I'm saying. A rhino smashed my Tomato-Mobile."

"And where is the rhino now? Hiding in the back of the truck?" the security guard asked.

One of the twins thumped the inside of the truck, making a bonking noise. Lin thumped the truck again, making it as obvious as possible, trying to cover up the noise.

"Oh no. That's impossible, now, isn't it? We got here a few seconds ago to check if everything was all right, and there are no rhinos in the back of this truck. That much I can tell you for sure," I said, telling the truth, but feeling guilty for not *really* telling the truth.

"I'm sure that boy is right," Mark said. "There's no

way you could fit a rhinoceros in the back of my Tomato-Mobile."

"Two baby T. rexes, sure. But not a rhinoceros," Lin said, not helping at all. The security guard gave her a little smile and a wink.

"Well, something happened here. I don't imagine a tomato truck can just flip itself over," the security guard said.

"Tomato-Mobile," Mark said. "It's a Tomato-Mobile."

"Right. I've got that written down now," the security guard said.

"Well, there was a big gust of wind a while back. Maybe it was the wind," I said.

"Or maybe a rhino escaped from the zoo, chased me through town, and then tried to flatten my tomato truck," Mark said.

"Your Tomato-Mobile," Lin corrected.

"Um, yeah. That's what I said," the driver said.

A dinosaur growled quietly from inside the truck.

"Oh. Sorry. I haven't eaten all day. I've been saving up for some festival food. Darn my growly stomach," Lin said with a grin.

"You should try the corn dogs, young lady.

They are so good they don't need ketchup," the security guard said.

"Thanks. I will," Lin said. She rubbed her stomach and growled.

The security guard took a step closer to the Tomato-Mobile and was about to have a look inside, when someone screamed behind us.

"That sounded like it was over by the food tents," Lin said, pointing with both hands toward the sound.

"It did," Mark said. "I bet it's the rhino!"

"Okay, Mark. Let's go look for the rhino. Then we'll call a tow truck and get your Tomato-Mobile flipped back over," the security guard said. "And you two better be moving along, too."

"We will. Have a nice day. Watch out for charging rhinoceroses," Lin said as the driver and the security guard ran toward the food tents.

I looked at Lin. "Come on. Let's go. We have to get to Bruno before they do," I said. I took a step, hoping to get there before the security guard, but Lin grabbed my shirt and pulled me back.

"What are you doing?" I asked.

She smiled and pointed in the opposite direction, away from the food tents and toward the fairgrounds. That's when I saw him. Bruno was staring down a garbage dumpster that had been recently coated in a bright red layer of paint.

# CHAPTER 5
# CHASING TROUBLE

Before we ran after Bruno, we let the twins out of the Tomato-Mobile. They looked like they were enjoying the snug little space, but when Lin instructed them to go round up Bruno, their eyes flashed with excitement. They might not be very good at staying put, but

the twins were excellent at herding Microsaurs.

Pizza and Cornelia burst away, sniffing the ground and tracking Bruno down. Lin and I chased after them as they ran through the parking lot, but there was no way we could keep up. When they were only a few feet away from

Bruno, he noticed them approaching. He stood still for a few seconds, and then it looked as if he was showing off or something, because he reared up on his back feet, lowered his big powerful crest, then charged into the big red dumpster.

The loud clang rang through the air and echoed off the stadium. The music in the concert was too loud for anyone inside to hear, although I was sure that the security guard would come running to check things out. But it was Pizza and Cornelia that got the worst of it. They had never heard anything so loud in their lives, and they completely forgot Lin's commands to round up Bruno as they ran off into the carnival booths like a couple of scared kittens.

"You go after Bruno," Lin said as she tapped on the Invisible Communicator. "And I'll go find the twins."

"Sounds good," I said as we split up. Lin and I usually work better together, but desperate times call for desperate measures. It's always good we can stay in touch, though. I made a mental note to thank my dad for the one hundredth time for inventing the little ear devices.

Bruno was thrashing the dumpster to the beat of the music when I arrived. I had to shout three times to get his attention. I was worried that he'd run, but he actually looked really happy to see me. His tail was wagging so much that his entire backside twisted back and forth, and his tongue drooped out of his mouth, wagging a little, too.

"Hey, big guy. How are you doing? Are you okay?" I asked in my most soothing voice.

Bruno hopped from foot to foot, turned, and nudged the garbage dumpster with the side of his crest.

"Yup. That's right. You're doing a great job smashing that big red dumpster. But I was wondering if you could just take it down a notch?" I took a few steps closer to Bruno, holding out my hand in front of me. I was only a foot away from reaching his nose horn. Bruno chuffed a little bark, then grinned.

"For sure. You're having quite a day, aren't you?" Bruno nodded and chuffed again. "Hey,

bud. How about you sit and we can work this out, okay?"

Bruno plopped his big backside down. His tail was still wagging so much that he made a little dust cloud behind him.

"That's a good boy. What do you say you and I head back to the Microterium? We'll get you a nice stick covered in peanut butter, and give you a big old belly rub," I said. I grabbed on to his nose horn. It was scuffed and scratched with red paint. Actually, his whole

crest was covered in nicks and dents. I clicked on my earbud and spoke to Lin.

"Hey, Lin. I think I figured something out," I said.

"This better be about how to get two Microsaurus rexes out of the merry-go-round," Lin said.

"Well, it was going to be about why Bruno was attacking red things, but I guess that can wait," I said. "How's it going?"

"Uh. Merry-go-round. Twins. Not so great," Lin said. I could tell she'd been running because she was breathing really hard. "You?"

I reached around and put my hand on Bruno's back. He was calming down a little, and I was going to jump on his back and start riding him, but something caught his eye. Bruno stood up, his eyes got a dangerous look in them, and then he tilted his head and charged.

"Oh man. I was going to say good, but guess who just found the bumper cars?" I said.

"Oh boy. That sounds like trouble," Lin said. "Hey, Pizza. Climb down from that giraffe!"

I was picturing Pizza and Cornelia climbing around on the merry-go-round animals as I ran after the charging triceratops. But even the images in my mind couldn't hold up to what I saw next. Bruno had climbed inside the bumper car ride. The polished cement floor was slippery so that the cars could glide around with ease. It made driving the bumper cars a lot of fun, and it also made it pretty entertaining to watch Bruno. His wide, flat feet weren't built for slippery conditions, and he kept falling down, doing the splits, rolling around, then fumbling back up on his feet as he tried to attack the cars.

Each car had a red light on its hood, and each time Bruno made contact with one of the cars, the light would blink on and a siren would wind up. The large puppy-saurus was having the time of his life as he skidded around on the slick floor, banging into lit-up cars. He was having so much fun that I wished he could stay there smashing cars until he was all pooped out. But that wasn't going to happen. In fact, the way I saw it, we probably only had another thirty minutes or so before the concert was over and the whole place would be flooded with people.

I had to think fast. There was no way I was going to convince Bruno to leave the bumper cars with their flashing red lights. It would be like trying to get a kitten out of a yarn-and-feathers factory. So I needed to do something about those red lights first.

I ran around to the back side of the bumper car attraction. I didn't know what I was looking for until I saw it. Just above my head there was a black box with a large lever on the side of it. Recognizing the power box, I jumped up, grabbed the handle, and yanked it down. The sirens stopped, though I could still hear Bruno crashing around inside the bumper car ride. I ran back to the front and saw Bruno bumping his head lightly against a car, looking a little sad that it wasn't flashing red anymore.

"Sorry, buddy. But trust me, it's for your own good," I said. I walked up to him on the slippery, polished cement floor and put my arm around his back.

Bruno sighed and let out a big breath. He'd had quite a day already.

"Okay, Bruno. It's time to go home," I said, and the big puppy-saurus licked my face with a tongue the size of a pillow.

I tapped on my Invisible Communicator. "Hey, Lin. I think he's ready to go back. He looks exhausted," I said.

"Shhh! Whisper. The security guard saw us and chased us into the carnival games area. We're trapped. We need a distraction. NOW!" she shout-whispered.

"On second thought, how would you like to rescue Lin first?" I asked the not-so-tiny-triceratops, and he gave me a little chuff. "I'll take that as a yes."

# CHAPTER 6
## FUN AND GAMES

I was so terrified that Bruno was going to run away at the first red cup, straw, or fleck of dust he saw that I walked backward right in front of his face. I didn't *actually* cover his eyes with my hands, but I did hold them out, spread my fingers, and wiggle them a lot to distract him. It seemed to be working, but it wasn't the fastest way to travel.

I led Bruno between a long line of empty carnival games, but the farther I got down the aisle, the more excited he got. It was impossible to keep him from seeing red in a place like this. Impossible.

I was thinking about how I was ever going to get out of this place without being discovered when I heard something behind the Plinko game tent.

"Pssst! Danny. Over here," Lin said. I looked and saw her and the twins peeking out from behind the tent. She motioned for us to come.

"Come on, Bruno. Go right

in there," I said as I turned Bruno's head toward the little alleyway between the tents. He wasn't so sure he wanted to go into the cramped space, but I pushed him from behind and he inched in. He got about halfway down the alley, then stopped.

"Lin," I said in my Invisible Communicator. "Grab his horn and pull. He's stuck."

I could hear Lin grunting as she yanked on Bruno's horn, and I gave him another big push with my shoulder. From my position behind the wedged-in triceratops, I had a good view down the carnival games aisle. However, what I viewed was not good. The security guard and Mark, the Tomato-Mobile driver, were heading our way. In a panic, I pushed with everything I had, and Bruno popped through the alley just before they saw me and his wide rump.

"That was close," Lin said. The twins were

staring at Bruno like he had just done something amazing. They were studying the scraps and nicks on his crest and horns, and I swear I saw Pizza nod as if he was pretty impressed.

"Yeah, but we're not out of danger yet. They are coming this way," I said.

"Oh man. We should just show them the Microsaurs and give ourselves up. Maybe if we only tell a few people they will help us keep the secret," Lin said.

"Actually, that's not a half-bad idea," I said.

"Really? Which half is good, then?" Lin asked.

"The show them the Microsaurs part," I said.

"You're crazy. I was kidding. Let's make a run for it," Lin said.

"It's too late. But I have a plan. There is about a one percent chance that it will work, but it's our best bet," I said. "Follow me. All of you."

I sprinted as fast as I could behind the

carnival game tents in the opposite direction
of Mark and the security guard. I passed the
dart game, the baseball throw, the dunking
booth. I even passed the milk-can toss and the
basketball hoop.

"Are we going to hide?" Lin asked.

"Yup," I said.

"Where?" Lin asked.

I found the booth I was looking for and
stopped. "Right here, in plain sight," I said.

"Um, I think you've lost your marbles, Danny,"
Lin said. "They'll see us for sure."

"That's the plan. I hope it works," I said. "Help
me lift this up, will ya?"

Lin and I lifted the back flap of the tent up as
high as we could, and then we encouraged the
Microsaurs to enter the ring toss carnival game.
I peeked around the edge and saw our visitors
heading our way. We only had a minute, maybe a
minute and a half, so we had to act fast.

I looked the twins right in the eyes and used my most commanding voice. "Sit!" I said, and to my surprise, they both sat. I looked at Lin and she gave me a thumbs-up. "Bruno, you sit over here," I said, pointing toward the front of the booth.

"Okay, now you three Microsaurs, listen up. If you have ever sat still in your entire life, this is the time. I need you to act like statues. If you wiggle, we're done. Caught. Kaput. Ruined! Do you understand?" I asked.

"I don't think they understand, Danny," Lin said.

"It's our only hope," I said. "Now, Lin, quick, pull down those stuffed animals and pile them up around the twins." I took another look at the driver and security guard heading toward us. We had thirty seconds max.

I grabbed a few rings from a small table, then jumped over the little barrier that separated the carnival games from the festival crowd.

"Step right up, step right up. Take your chance at landing a ring on the super-fake, absolutely not real one little bit dinosaur horn and win a prize," I said.

The driver and the security guard were
surprised to see me. I was pretty sure they thought
they were alone. Well, except for the runaway
rhino they were probably still searching for.

"What are you doing here?" the guard asked with her hands on her hips. "And where's your little friend?"

"Oh. Me. I'm right here, just making sure the prizes are looking good," Lin said as she tucked a big pink teddy bear between Pizza's and Cornelia's heads. "There. That's perfect."

"Okay. There you are, but now the question is double. What are you two doing here?"

"Oh, we're doing a research paper on how it would be to work in a carnival. Larry, the normal ring toss operator guy, said we could help out while the concert was going," Lin said.

"A research paper?" Mark asked. "In the summer?"

I looked at Lin. She looked as confused as the driver and as worried as me. She was out of

answers, so shrugged it off to me. I thought quick and spit out the first thing that came to mind.

"Um, yeah. It's not for school. It's for, uh, um . . . a contest. Yeah. That's it," I said.

"All right. I'll try it," the driver said. "How much is the prize?"

"One hundred thousand dollars," Lin said.

"One hundred thousand dollars?" the driver asked. "Are you out of your mind? Give me those rings."

"Wait, that's not really the prize," I said.

"I know, kid. I know how this gig works. Stand back."

The squatty little driver in his puffy tomato hat ripped the rings out of my hands and tossed one over my head. It landed perfectly on Bruno's top left horn. I'll admit, it was a pretty good shot.

"Not bad," the security guard said.

"You haven't seen anything yet," the driver said. "My mom was a carny. I grew up on these games." He tossed the second ring without even looking. This one  landed on the other horn with ease.

"This guy is too good," Lin whispered in my ear. "We might be in trouble here."

"We've been in trouble all day. What's new?" I said.

The driver tossed an underhand throw and the third ring spun perfectly in the air before it landed on Bruno's nose horn. Mark smirked, then took a bow.

"Thank you, thank you," he said, then spun

around and looked right at me. "And now, for my prize."

"Um, yeah. About that," I said.

"I'd like the realistic-looking stuffed dinosaur. It'd look great in my man cave," he said with a smile.

"Sorry. Those are part of the decorations. If we even thought about giving those away, we'd lose our jobs," Lin said.

"I thought you were volunteering for some project or something," the driver said. "I think something fishy is going on here."

"All right. That's enough, Mark. Let's keep moving. We have to find your runaway rhinoceros, remember," the security guard said. "Good luck with your project, you two. And stay out of trouble."

"We always do," Lin said, telling the biggest lie she's ever told in her entire life.

We waited until they were out of sight, and then we both breathed a huge sigh of relief.

"I can't believe that worked," Lin said.

"Me neither." I looked over at Bruno. He had a ring around each of his horns and a big smile on his face. Pizza and Cornelia were starting to lose patience, and as they stood up, all the stuffed animal prizes fell to the ground.

"You know, I've seen the Microsaurs do some amazing things, but sitting still for this long has to be the most incredible thing yet," Lin said.

"I completely agree," I said.

"Come on. Let's go," Lin said. "I've had enough of this festival for the day."

I was about to agree when I looked down the aisle again. A small crowd of people had gathered at the end. I looked in the other direction only to see even more people walking our way from that side. And to make matters worse, most of them were dressed in red from head to toe.

"Oh man. We're doomed," I said. "Bruno is going to go nuts with all these red tomato festival T-shirts and hats."

Lin noticed the people, too. "What? The concert isn't over. I can still hear the music thumping inside the stadium."

"It must be the carnival games workers. They are setting up early. Getting ready for the crowds," I said.

"We need another distraction," Lin said.

"We need a Vicky Van-Varbles," I said.

# CHAPTER 7
# LEADING THE BLIND

"There's no way she's going to hear us. She's probably onstage waving a tomato flag or something at this very moment," Lin said as I tapped my Invisible Communicator on.

"It's worth a try," I said. "Maybe she can make the concert last longer or something."

"What? Who? I can barely hear you," Vicky said in my ear. Of course, there was also a rock concert in my ear now as well.

"I can't believe you heard us! Vicky, we need your help," Lin said.

"Hang on. One sec," Vicky said, then the concert got quieter in our earpieces. She said "excuse me" five times in the next six seconds, and then I heard a door slam shut and the concert was only a small thud in my ears again. "Is that better?"

"Much. Thanks, Vicky. It's so good to hear your voice," I said.

"It really is," Lin agreed.

"Really? Well, that's nice. It's good to hear you guys as well. Are you enjoying the show? Aren't the Ruby Girls just the BEST?!" she said, and I could almost see her smile in my mind.

"Um, well, that's a long story, but let's just say we've been up to our eyeballs in emergencies and we haven't really had a chance to hear the Ruby Girls much," I explained.

"Oh no. I hope everything is okay. I can't think of anything that would make me miss this concert," Vicky said.

"We're glad you're having fun. And that's why we are calling actually," Lin said. "How much longer is the concert?"

"Oh. They are on their last song now. Sorry, Lin. I'm guessing you're too late," Vicky said.

"Do you think you could stretch it out a little? Maybe talk them into one last encore or something?" I asked.

"Funny you should ask, Danny. And I guess the

secret is safe now, and I *really* wish you two were here to see it, but there is one last number and it is super special. I'm sure my dad will record it. Which reminds me. I gotta run," Vicky said.

"Wait. Before you go. We need more than just help stretching out the concert. We need a place

to hide three Microsaurs before the crowd sees them," I said.

"What? That's not a big deal. Put them in your pocket," Vicky said, which totally made sense given that she had no idea Bruno, Pizza, and Cornelia were giant-sized.

"That's not gonna work. There was an accident at the Microterium and now Bruno is the size of a truck," Lin said.

"What? Oh my gosh. I want to see him!" Vicky said.

I could hear someone calling Vicky's name in the background. It must have been pretty loud because it was coming through my Invisible Communicator pretty clear.

"I'll have to see him later. I gotta run."

"Not yet! We have the twins, too, and they are massive. They look pretty scary to someone who doesn't know them," I said.

"Okay. I have an idea. Behind the stadium

there are three tour trucks. One is a bus, and the other two are big semitrucks. Run there, ask for a guy named Gino. Tell him Vicky sent you. He'll help you hide away the Microsaurs. I'll meet you there after the concert," Vicky said.

"But there's another problem," Lin said. "This whole place is covered in red. Even the people in the concert are wearing red shirts. Bruno is going to act like a wild bowling ball in a field of pins."

"Gotta go. You'll have to science your way out of this one, guys," Vicky said, then started warming up her voice, singing scales and doing funny breathing exercises.

"She sounds pretty good," I said, and Lin nodded.

"Not bad at all," Lin said.

"All right. We need to make a run for it," I said. "But first, I'm going to need that sign." I pointed to the top of the tent we were hiding behind. There was a blue banner, definitely not red, with the words *Ring Toss* written on it in white paint.

"I'm on it," Lin said. "Corney, I'm going to need your help."

Lin pushed Cornelia right up tight against the back of the tent, climbed on her back, and stepped carefully onto the Microsaurus rex's square head. Lin reached up as high as she could, but she was still a few inches from the banner.

"All right, girl. Give me a nudge," Lin said. Cornelia stretched up to her highest height and tilted her head up for that last little bit. Lin grabbed a handful of the banner

and then jumped. The string that was holding the banner in place ripped, and down came Lin with the sign in her hands. "Easy peasy," she said as she offered me the sign.

"For you," I said with a grin.

"What are you going to do with it?" Lin asked.

"What are *we* going to do with it, you mean," I said. "Take your end and follow me."

I was a little worried about what I was going to do next, but I knew it was the only way we were going to get Bruno out of here without him going into full-tilt-boogie-red-is-my-mortal-enemy-charge mode again. I explained to Lin that I needed her on one side of the big puppy-saurus while I took the other end of the banner around to Bruno's other side. I talked to him nice and slow as we carefully lowered the banner over his crest, then down over his eyes. Using the strings that once held the banner in place,

I tied the makeshift blindfold snuggly behind
Bruno's head. He wasn't so great with it at first,
but after I told him it was a game and that he'd
get a big peanut-buttery surprise when this was
all over, he seemed to trust me
enough to give it a shot.

Leading Bruno by holding on to his nose horn, Lin, Pizza, Cornelia, and I made our way toward the back of the stadium.

"This is pretty great, ya know?" Lin said.

"Are you serious?"

"Yes, I'm serious. I think it's exciting. We're sneaking around, trying not to be seen," Lin said.

"It isn't us I'm worried about being spotted. It's the two T. rexes and a blindfolded triceratops that worry me. One big blast of wind and this could turn into a disaster."

"Always the optimist," Lin said with a grin.

Walking behind the booths and any cover we could find, we worked our way out of the carnival games area. Pizza and Cornelia were starting to look bored, which wasn't a good sign at all, as we weaved our way behind a booth filled with T-shirts covered in tomato designs.

Lin popped out from behind the booth first, and she took a step back, holding her hands up to stop us all at once.

"Don't take another step," she said. "It's the door to the stadium, and people are starting to come out."

"How many?" I asked.

"It just looks like all the festival workers, so not that many, but does it really matter?" she asked.

"Uh, I guess not. Should we just make a run for it?" I asked.

Lin looked around as I felt the jitters creep up and down my back. This whole day had been a mess, and I was about to pull out my phone and call Professor Penrod for advice when Lin had an idea.

"Quick. Follow me," she said, bolting off in the opposite direction from the stadium. I didn't

even bother asking where we were going. I just
grabbed Bruno by the horn and ran.

Lin and the twins were much faster than
the two of us, and I watched as they ran toward
a strange-looking building with warped walls
and hundreds of tiny squares covering it that
reflected the sun and sky.

"The Hall of Mirrors?" I asked in my Invisible Communicator. "Are you sure that's a good idea?"

"Are you kidding? It's not only a shortcut to Vicky's hideaway semitruck, it's going to be fun, too," Lin said, then led the twins into the strange-looking building.

# CHAPTER 8
# THINGS ARE NOT
# HOW THEY APPEAR

"I can't see anything," Lin said as we fumbled around in the dark.

"Our eyes will adjust," I said. "I can see better already."

Compared to the bright summer sun outside, the Hall of Mirrors felt like entering an underground cave. It was cool and a little damp from the air cooler on the roof, and being packed in there with three large dinos certainly made it feel cramped.

"Oh yeah. There are tiny lights in the ceiling. They almost look like stars," Lin said. "This place is pretty cool."

"We don't have time for cool. We have to find the back door and get out of here," I said.

"If there is a back door. I didn't even think of that," Lin said. Lin led the way, walking through a door so short the twins had to duck to go in. I had to tilt Bruno's head one way, then the next to make our way through, and I started to panic as the white lights in the ceiling revealed that the floor and walls were painted bright red.

And if walking in a totally red hallway wasn't challenging enough, there were loads of things for Bruno to smash if he got a peek. At the end of the little hallway there was a trick mirror that made us look like we were squatty and short.

"We have to hurry and get out. This place makes me nervous," I said.

Lin started laughing. She puffed out her cheeks to make her reflection look even funnier, and the twins got into the act as well. "Oh man. I wish we could hang out here all day. This is hilarious," she said as she rubbed her chubby belly in the mirror and laughed again.

"We can come back when
we aren't outnumbered by
previously extinct, supersecret
Microsaurs."

"Deal," Lin said, before turning
the corner into the next hallway.

The little yellow lights in
the ceiling changed in the next
room, and there were more
mirrors. Fastened to taller
frames that reached all the way
to the ceiling were two long
mirrors. As we walked past,
we first looked really tall
then really short. The twins
were a little spooked by
the tall mirrors at first,
but when they saw Lin
laughing at herself they
decided it was okay.

"I need mirrors like this at my house. I feel so powerful," Lin said as she flexed her muscles in the mirror.

"Just wait until you try this one. You won't want one in your room anymore," I said as I pulled Bruno past the short reflection. "Come on. Let's keep going."

"This room is so yellow," Lin said. "I feel like I'm swimming in lemonade." She made swimming motions over to the next mirror, laughed at being so short, then swam on to the next room.

The lights in the ceiling turned green, and the mirrors made us look either super skinny or really fat. I'll admit, seeing a thin, blindfolded triceratops almost made me forget we were in so much trouble. I smiled, and almost laughed, then noticed

something that clicked an idea spark in my brain.

"Hang on a second. Wasn't the floor painted red in the other rooms?" I asked.

Lin looked down between her feet. "Yeah. It's gray in here. It's no big deal, Danny."

"It might be. It might be a very big deal. Do you have anything that is red?" I asked Lin. She thought for a second, and then an idea spark clicked in her mind as well. She pulled something out of her back pocket and showed it to

me. It was the tomato lollipop she had purchased before our wild adventures began for the day.

She was grinning at first, but when she got a look at the color of her candy treat, her face turned angry. "What? I was saving this for later, but now it's ruined. It isn't red anymore. It's all gray!" she said.

"Actually, it isn't gray at all. It's still bright red," I said. For the first time in a while I was starting to feel some hope. Sure, we weren't much better than we were a few seconds ago, but I'd learned something pretty neat.

"Danny. This is not bright red," Lin said.

"Trust me, it is. But the even better news is that I figured out the solution to the Bruno-charging-red-stuff problem," I said.

Lin tilted her head at me. She looked totally confused, so I let her in on the plan.

"Come on, Lin. We need to get out of here and make a pair of triceratops-sized green goggles," I said.

"Great. And how is that going to fix my lollipop?" Lin asked.

"Follow me. Your lollipop will be fine," I said, feeling the tiniest bit better.

We made our way through a few more rooms, traveled through a hallway or two so narrow Bruno's crest scraped on each side, and then finally I found what I was searching for.

"Look. Under that door. It's sunlight trying to sneak in," I said.

"Oh good. I'm mad at this lollipop ruining the Hall of Mirrors anyway," Lin said. "Let's get out of here."

I hurried to the door, then pried it open. I heard the roar of the crowd before my eyes adjusted to the light again and they came into view. I shut the door as fast as I could. Lin and the Microsaurs were staring at me like I had lost my mind.

"Um. We *cannot* go out there. We're too late," I said.

"Crowds?" Lin asked.

"More like a mob," I said.

Lin reached up as calm as could be and tapped her ear. "Hey, Vicky. Can you hear us?" she asked. I didn't turn mine on. I wanted silence to think for a bit. Lin continued her one-sided conversation.

"Yeah. We're almost to the trailer, but we're stuck. There is a mob behind the stadium blocking our way," Lin said. "Uh-huh. Yes. Oh, I know. He tends to panic from time to time. What can you do?"

I had a feeling Lin and Vicky were talking about me, but I didn't have time to think about that. I was trying to get us out of the Hall of Mirrors before people joined us in the odd-shaped building.

"Yeah. A distraction is exactly what we need," Lin said. She listened for a while, nodding along with what Vicky was saying. "Oh yeah. That's perfect. Oh, I bet. You're so lucky."

Lin walked between the twins, scooted under Bruno, and smooshed her way between me and the big troublemaking triceratops. She motioned for me to move over, and I stepped away from the door.

"Okay. Sounds good. In three, two . . ." Lin started counting down, then opened the door wide and walked out confidently. "One. Thanks, Vicky. You're right. All this crowd needed was the Ruby Girls. A perfect distraction if I've ever seen one. See you in the semitruck in a few. Thanks again," Lin said.

She turned and looked over her shoulder at me. "What are you waiting for?" she asked.

"A miracle," I said. "And I guess the Ruby Girls just gave us one." I looked at the mob again. They were all crowding around five shiny, glittery singers as they waved pink and purple pads of paper, hoping for an autograph. Then, right in the middle of the Ruby Girls, I made eye contact with

the glitteriest of all the girls, and she gave me a
little wave. I don't know what was going on, but
it was Vicky, right there with her favorite band,
signing autographs along with them.

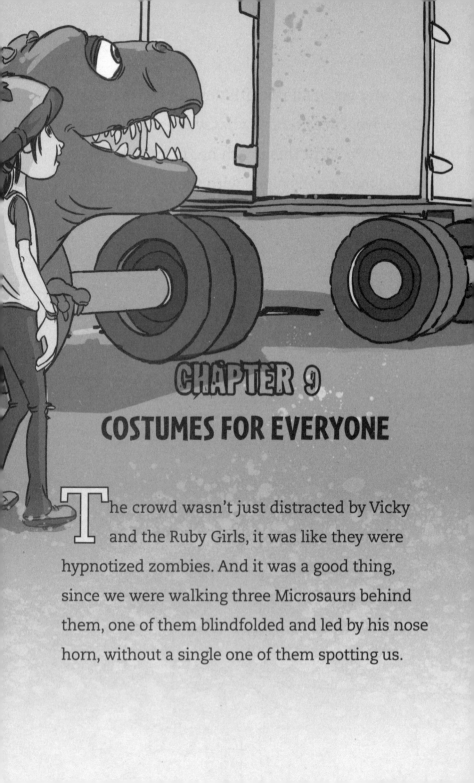

# CHAPTER 9
## COSTUMES FOR EVERYONE

The crowd wasn't just distracted by Vicky and the Ruby Girls, it was like they were hypnotized zombies. And it was a good thing, since we were walking three Microsaurs behind them, one of them blindfolded and led by his nose horn, without a single one of them spotting us.

"That was a total rush!" Lin said as we made our way to the big tour semitrucks parked behind the stadium.

"Which one do we go in?" I asked as we looked around.

"I have no idea," Lin said. "But it's not that one." She pointed to a large tour bus with a picture of the Ruby Girls on it.

"Let's go check that one," I said, pointing to a big black truck with a gray trailer the size of a house on it.

"That would be a bad idea," a voice said behind us, and I felt my heart thumping in my chest. Heck, it was thumping so hard I could feel it in my eyeballs.

Lin, Bruno, Pizza, Cornelia, and I turned around slowly. The little man standing behind us was dressed in a pair of overalls. He had a tool belt around his waist, a big mustache that looked like a push broom, and he was wearing a little red hat.

"I swear, if you tell me your name is Mario, I'm going to pass out," Lin said.

"Ha. I get that a lot actually. Sorry to disappoint you. I'm just Gino," he said. A wide grin spread across his face, showing a gap between his front teeth. Then his eyes opened wide, and I thought he was going to run.

"Wait. Vicky told us to find you. We can explain everything," I said in a hurry.

"Oh. It's okay. Miss Van-Varbles already explained, but I have to admit: When she said the robotic puppet dinosaurs were realistic, I thought she was exaggerating.

These are amazing," he said. He reached out a hand and touched Pizza's nose. The Microsaurus rex bared his teeth and growled at Gino.

"That's enough, Pizza," Lin said in a calm voice.

"Oh my. His name is Pizza? That's wonderful. Pizza is my favorite food," Gino said. "But for now, follow me. We need to hide you guys before everyone sees you. We don't want to ruin the surprise."

"What surprise?" Lin asked.

"Ha ha. You two are as funny as Miss Van-Varbles promised as well. What surprise? *What surprise?*"

We followed Gino to the back of the *correct* semitruck, and he knocked on the door three times. *RAP-RAP-RAP!* Someone from inside returned the knock, and then the back door swung wide open. Gino pulled a small metal staircase down from the back of the truck and motioned for us to enter.

"After you, my new friends," he said.

We climbed inside the truck. It fit all of us, but just barely. It wasn't that it wasn't big enough. It was plenty big. It was that it was filled with glittery, feathery, leathery costumes. Bolts and bolts of fancy material lined one wall, and mirrors, normal mirrors, not strange ones like in the Hall of Mirrors, lined the others.

It looked like we were alone in the strange place until I heard someone humming to herself from behind an army of half-bodied mannequins dressed in fancy rock concert clothes. An older woman, no taller than Lin, emerged. She pushed her glasses up on the bridge of her nose, saw the creatures standing in her costume closet, and dropped a bag of snacks she'd been holding.

"Oh my. You startled me," the woman said.

"Kathleen, this is, well, I don't know who it is actually, but they are guests of Miss Van-Varbles," Gino said.

"I'm Lin and this is Danny," Lin said. "Nice to meet you."

"And you. And you've brought some friends," Kathleen said. "Some large friends."

"Oh, don't worry about those. They are just puppets," Gino said.

"Nonsense. I know a puppet when I see one," the costume lady said. She turned and started looking through the cloth. "Too blue, I think," she said, talking her way through the images in her mind. "And not enough of this, although I believe pink is your color," she said to Cornelia, and the T. rex grinned.

"Um, are you all right?" Gino asked. "Because I need to check on the hitch for the parade float. Want to make sure it's in tip-top shape for the girls."

"Oh, quite, Gino. Honestly, I'm not sure how you could help if you did stay. Run along, we'll get our guests costumed in no time," Kathleen said.

"Costumed?" I asked.

"Of course. If you go to a baker, don't you expect bread?" the little woman said as she pulled a massive swatch of purple cloth down from a shelf. "This will do nicely."

"Yeah, but," Lin started in. Gino jumped out of the back of the truck and Kathleen turned to watch him leave. He closed the door and Kathleen smiled at us with a knowing grin.

"What? Did we do something wrong?" I asked.

"On the contrary. In fact, you've just made me a very happy woman," she said, then did something I did not expect. Kathleen flipped up the collar of her shirt, and a shiny silver pin reflected in the overhead lights of the traveling costume shop. It was round, had a drawing of

Bruno on it, and had the letters *IMPA* stamped around its edge.

"Holy moly. You're a member of the International Microsaur Protection Agency?" I asked, my mind blown.

"Charter member number one hundred and eleven," she said proudly. "And I've been expecting your visit for some time now. In fact, we all have."

"Who? Is Gino a member of the IMPA, too?" Lin asked.

"Oh no. Not Gino. But he's helpful and a really good mechanic. He can build anything you can dream up. Handy, and kind of cute if you ask me," she said. She winked at Lin, and it made her giggle.

"Then who is 'we'?" I asked. "You said 'we' were waiting for us to arrive."

Kathleen motioned for us to follow her back farther into the costume room. We wound our way past sewing machines, flat tables, and more cloth than I'd seen in my life, until we reached her drawing table. There, sitting on a small tripod, was none other than Professor Penrod. Okay, it was a cell phone, but on the other end of the camera phone, the good professor was looking into the camera, waving right at us.

"Well, are you going to say hello, you two, or are you just going to hang around and visit with my sister, Kathleen? The finest seamstress in the entire world. And a peach of a Microsaur explorer as well," Professor Penrod said.

"I may be freaking out here a little," I said.

"Well, make sure you pick out a nice hat before you do. I'm fond of the feathered ones, myself," Professor Penrod said.

"That's odd. I seem to remember you being fond of the grass hats, Penny," Kathleen said. "In fact, I remember making you a full grass suit or two in my time."

"Okay. Now I'm freaking out," Lin said. "You
made his grass suit?"

"Oh, and you should see his tree bark
swimming suit. Now, that is a sight to behold,"
Kathleen said. "Isn't that right, Penny?"

"I have no idea what you are talking about," he said, but I could tell by the look on his face that he knew exactly what his sister was talking about, and now I couldn't get the picture out of my mind.

# CHAPTER 10
## SEEING THINGS IN A NEW SHADE

W hile Kathleen took every measurement imaginable of Lin, the Microsaurs, and me, we told Dr. Carlyle and Penrod about our close calls. Now that we were in the safety of the costume truck, it was kind of fun to think about how the day had gone.

"I can't believe you didn't get caught," Dr. Carlyle said.

"Fine thinking on your feet to cover Bruno's eyes," Professor Penrod said.

"And who would have thought that sneaking through a Hall of Mirrors with three Microsaurs was even possible?" Kathleen said.

"I know, right? And then Danny told me he had an idea of how to get Bruno out of here without him charging red. Right, Danny?" Lin said.

"Well, yes, but we don't need that anymore," I said.

"Why not?" Lin asked.

"Because we're safe in the truck. They can just drive us out of here and drop us off at the Microterium. We'll shrink them back to size and we're back to normal," I said.

"Oh, but that's not the plan at all," Professor Penrod said.

"Why not? That actually sounds like a great idea," Lin said.

"Penny and I already discussed it, and it just seems too risky. Gino isn't a problem. He'll believe just about anything he hears. But if we need to get the truck driver and the Ruby Girls' manager involved so we can borrow the truck, then we'd probably need the Ruby Girls themselves. Well, you can see that before long there would be a pretty big group involved, and before long our secret wouldn't be so secret anymore," Kathleen said.

"Yeah. I guess that makes sense," I said. "But how are we going to get out of here, then? We're still stuck!"

"Yeah, do we just wait in here until the whole festival is over?" Lin asked.

"We could do that, but then this would go to waste," Kathleen said as she stood up from her sewing machine. She was carrying something that looked like a blanket, made of the glitteriest fabric I'd ever seen. She walked past me and right up to Cornelia, and she tickled the Microsaurus rex's chin. "Bring your head down here, pretty girl," she said, then, as Cornelia obeyed, the tiny costume lady flung the cloth over the T. rex's back. Then she pulled on two strings, and one edge of the costume pulled up over Cornelia's head and eyes, and turned her into a sparkly, masked superhero dinosaur.

"Oh my goodness. It's ADORABLE!" Lin said.

"Thank you. I'll admit, I'm pretty proud of this one. I'm thinking her brother here should have a matching costume, but he'd look dashing in emerald green," Kathleen said.

"Or aqua blue," Lin said. "It'd bring out his eyes."

"Right you are, Miss Lin. Right you are, and I have just the stuff. Come on, I'll need your help to get it down."

Lin and Kathleen scurried toward a shelf of bluish-green material, but I still had no idea what was going on.

"Um. What is going on? We can't superhero our way out of this," I said.

"Don't you see, Danny? We're getting costumes," Lin said.

"Yeah. I can see that, but why?" I asked.

"So we can march in the parade. Isn't it obvious?" Lin said, then reached up and pulled down some aqua material.

"You're telling me we're going to dress up the Microsaurs and march right out of here like it's no big deal?" I said.

"Exactly, Danny. Hiding in plain sight is the name of the operation today," Professor Penrod said from the camera phone.

"Well, then I'm going to need to go visit Gino," I said.

"Why?" Lin asked.

"Because I need a pair of green goggles big enough to fit a triceratops, and I need them fast," I said.

"Oh, that'd be perfect for his costume. Now you get it, Danny," Lin said.

"Actually, it's a complementary color thing. You see, Bruno has this habit where he charges everything red he sees. If I can get him to wear green glasses, everything red will appear gray. No more red, no more charging. So, where do I find Gino?" I asked Kathleen.

"He's in the next trailer over. It's his tinker truck, and if you need goggles welded together, that is the perfect place to start," Kathleen said.

"Hurry back, Danny," Lin said. "I'll pick you out something nice to wear." She put a feather scarf around her neck and a pink hat on her head.

"Oh great. Now I'm afraid," I said.

I squirmed past the patiently waiting
Microsaurs, out the back door of the costume shop,
and ran over to Gino's tinker truck. I rapped on the
back door three times, RAP-RAP-RAP, then waited.
It seemed like it took forever, but three raps came
back, and then the back door swung open.

Gino was wearing large gloves and a welding
helmet. He flipped up the visor and looked down

at me. "Well, hello there, young man. You look like you need some help."

"How did you know?" I asked.

"Honestly, knocking on my door always means someone needs help. It's what I do. I help," he said, then lowered a gloved hand and helped me into his truck.

"Well, I'd be lying if I said I didn't need help. I

hope that's all right," I said as I got a first glance at his truck. "Oh man. This place is awesome."

Gino beamed with pride. "I'm glad you think so. Not everyone can appreciate my idea of organizing things," he said.

There were piles and stacks of metal and boards all over the place. The room had gears, wires, glass light bulbs, long tubes of metal and brass. There were stone steps, iron hammers, welding equipment, and more tools than I could count.

"I love it. My dad is an inventor, so I've been around workshops my entire life. This is perfect," I said.

"The son of an inventor, eh? Well, then I'm sure you have more than just a need. I bet you have a plan," the small, mustached man said.

"You bet I do," I said as I spied a chalkboard screwed to the wall of the rolling toolshed. "Can I use that?"

Gino pulled off one huge glove, then dug deep into an oversized pocket. He pulled out his hand and offered me a piece of chalk. "I can't wait to see what you have up your sleeve," he said.

"Arms," I replied, and we both laughed.

I drew my idea for Bruno's goggles on the board. Luckily, while Kathleen had done her measurements I'd paid close attention, and I added them to the drawing as well. The handyman and I discussed a few details, he made some suggestions, and then we got to work.

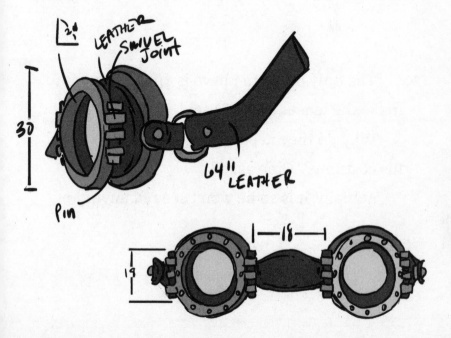

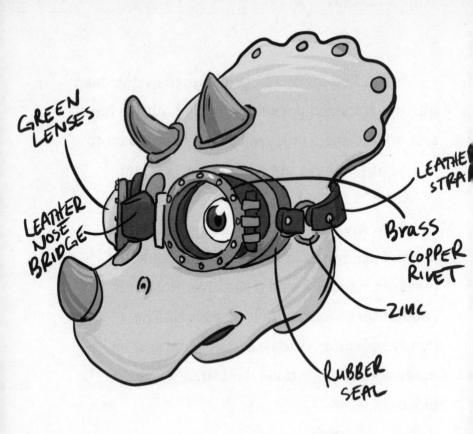

GREEN
LENSES

LEATHER
NOSE
BRIDGE

LEATHER
STRAP

Brass

COPPER
RIVET

ZINC

RUBBER
SEAL

"The only problem I have is knowing what to make the lenses out of," I said.

"Why do they need to be green? Is it to match his costume?" Gino asked.

"Actually, it is so he won't see red anymore.

You see, when Bruno sees the color red, he goes nutso. If we can make him look through green goggles, then all the red will just look gray. We tested it in the Hall of Mirrors," I said.

"Well, if you say so. You're the inventor," Gino said. He sparked up his welder, and a little blue flame sputtered to life. "In a drawer over there labeled 'Gels' you'll find every color you can imagine. Find the right shade of green and we'll get going."

I found the big sheets of colored plastic gels exactly where Gino said they would be, and sure enough, he had the perfect shade of green. I helped him find scraps and parts for our project, and we took turns welding, cutting, and assembling until we had the perfect pair of Bruno glasses in our hands.

"So. Do you think these will work?" Gino asked.

"Are you kidding? They are perfect. I can't wait to try them on my dinosaur," I said.

"You mean your dinosaur puppet, right?" Gino said.

"Um, yeah. My puppet. Right," I said. "Thanks again, Gino."

I flung the goggles over my shoulder and jumped down out of the truck. I was halfway to the costume truck when Gino leaned out the door and hollered after me.

"Hey, Danny. I'm confused again. If Bruno, as you call him, is a puppet, then why does he need glasses to keep him from charging red?"

I stopped dead in my tracks. "Um. Because Bruno has a complicated artificial intelligence computer controlling him, and one time there was a lightning storm and it fried his circuitry, and then . . ."

Gino winked and waved. "Don't worry, son. Your secret is safe with me," he said, then closed the door to his tinker truck.

# CHAPTER 11
## TALK ABOUT A MAKEOVER

"Danny. Hurry. It's an emergency," Lin's voice said in my Invisible Communicator as I arrived at the costume truck.

"I'm here. Open the door. What's wrong?" I asked in a panic. In a flash I imagined the worst. Maybe the Microsaurs had escaped again. Perhaps the Ruby Girls had returned to the truck and discovered Bruno and the twins. What if Bruno's blindfold had slipped off and he'd gone bananas in the back of the truck, tearing every scrap of red material into shreds? But nothing prepared me for what I saw when Lin opened the back door of Kathleen's costume truck.

"Is that your real hair?" I asked. Lin's hair was so bright pink that I had to blink a few times before I could focus on it. She had two puff balls of hair poking up from either side of her head. "And are those glitter freckles?"

"Rrrgh!" Lin growled with her teeth gritted tight.

"I told you. Pink is totally your color," Vicky said.

"One word and I will never speak to you again," Lin said. Vicky was behind her with a large suitcase full of makeup. Kathleen was pinning a massive silky saddle thing on Bruno's back. But Lin was the real shocker.

"Actually," I said as I climbed in the truck, "you look like a real Ruby Girl."

I knew that was the wrong thing to say.

"It's a wig, Danny, and if you know what's good for you you'll stop talking right now," Lin said, then growled again.

"You look totally punk rock," I corrected myself. "I'm serious."

This softened Lin a little, but there was still a ways to go before she would be back to normal.

"I told her she looked like a real Ruby Girl, too," Vicky said, and Lin growled AGAIN. "It's a compliment, Lin. Really."

"This isn't helping, Vicky," I said.

"Well, maybe this will," Vicky said with an excited grin. "You're next."

"Oh no. I don't think so," I said. "Besides, I need to try on Bruno's goggles."

"There's no way those will fit. They are too big for you," Kathleen said. I was about to correct her when I noticed she was joking.

"Help me out?" I asked Lin, handing her one side of the massive goggles. She took it and blinked, and I noticed she had long fake eyelashes on. I didn't say a word about them.

"So, what's up with the goggles?" Vicky asked.

"They will make it so he won't see red," I said.

"More like, he won't charge red," Lin said.

"That's the hope." I walked around Bruno, rubbing his backside as I made the journey. "It's okay, boy. It's just me, and I bet you want this thing off, don't you?"

"Is he ready?" Lin asked.

"We have to do it fast. In one movement," I said. "We pull off the blindfold, then put the glasses on as fast as possible."

"Wait. I have an idea," Vicky said. "You two get the glasses ready. You know, hold them right over his eyes, and I'll yank the blindfold off. That way all you need to do is basically drop them in place."

"Great. Let's do it," I said.

Vicky climbed on Bruno's back and untied the blindfold behind his wide crest, and Lin and I balanced the new green goggles above his head.

"Okay. On the count of three," Lin said. "One, two, THREE!"

Vicky yanked, and Lin and I dropped. Then we swung the straps back to Vicky, and she fastened the big buckle in the back behind Bruno's head. The big, lovable puppy-saurus looked around the room, his round eyes blinking behind a thin layer of glass and green plastic gels. As he tried to figure out his surroundings, Kathleen was petting Pizza and feeding him a leftover hamburger while Cornelia tore the stuffing out of a pillow. I was worried that he was going to panic and start charging the place into a pile of rubble, but something about seeing his friends enjoying the place must have worked, because Bruno lolled his tongue out of his mouth and smiled.

"Hey. He likes them," Lin said.

"Thank goodness," I agreed.

"And he looks so cute I could just squeeze him," Vicky said.

"Go ahead. He'd like that, too. Group hug," I said, and the three of us surrounded Bruno and gave him the best hug ever. Even Kathleen joined in, which didn't surprise me being that she was the sister of a famous micro-paleontologist.

We hugged and laughed and told Bruno how great he was for a bit, and then Vicky caught on to my game.

"Hey. You did that to stall. You don't want me to do your makeup," she said. She was 100 percent correct. I shrugged my shoulders. "Well, too bad, mister. Up in the chair."

Vicky pointed to a chair next to the mirrors. There was no arguing with her now. She had that getting-down-to-business look in her eyes that let me know there was no way I was getting out of this.

Lin laughed and made horrible suggestions while Vicky covered my face with makeup. She put stuff around my eyes. She patted powder on my cheeks. She even put something I swear was blue glue in my hair and combed it up into a pretty tall Mohawk. And while she was doing all this stuff, Kathleen was busy in the back, hunched over her sewing machine, making something for us to wear.

Vicky stood back from me in the makeup chair. She put her hands on her hips, tilted her head, and thought for a second. She went to her bag, pulled out three tubes of lipstick, and held them up to the light. She selected one and looked at Lin, and Lin shook her head.

"Guys. All this silence is freaking me out," I said. They just smiled while Lin pointed to one of the lipsticks Vicky held up. Vicky nodded in agreement, took the cap off the lipstick, then moved in for the final touches.

"*Magnifique!*" Vicky said. "Ready to see the masterpiece?"

"No. Not even one little bit," I said. I'd been turned away from the mirror the entire time, but it looked like that was coming to an end.

Vicky swiveled my chair around, and I saw a stranger in the mirror. Lin and Vicky crowded around me, joining me in the mirror. At first I didn't know what to think, and then I relaxed as I realized something amazing.

"You know. I look awesome," I said as I watched the grin in the other me in the mirror show my white teeth.

"Yes you do," Lin said. "And now that I see us both together, I have to say we both look pretty punk rock."

"Just wait till you see me," Vicky said. "Out of the chair, Danny. It's my turn."

While Vicky did her own makeup and hair, Kathleen fitted us into our new costumes. We looked like superhero punk rockers that had an accident in a glitter factory. It wasn't something I would wear to school, but dressing up in something totally different felt great. Vicky got dressed in her new outfit. And the three of us

posed for a few pictures with the costumed Microsaurs for Kathleen. We even talked her into taking a selfie with us. Then Vicky's phone rang.

"Oh, hi, girls. Yes. We're almost ready. Is it time for the parade?" Vicky said into the phone.

"Well, we're not going to fit on the actual float with you, but I promise we'll be a sight you won't forget. I thought we could just walk alongside of the float and wave." Vicky paused as the person, or people by the sound of it, responded. "Sure. Great. Be there in a jiffy. Love ya, and remember, RG forever!"

"RG forever?" I asked. "Who was that?"

"Oh, that was my girls," she said as if it were no big deal. "My Ruby Girls, that is."

"How do you know them so well?" Lin asked. "I mean. You introduced them in the concert, and you were with them signing autographs."

"Oh, and you guys missed my special musical number," she said. "But don't worry. My dad recorded it. And so did everyone else with a camera phone, I bet."

"Sheesh. It's like you're one of them," I said.

"Well, not exactly, but you never know.

However, this will probably give you a clue,"
Vicky said. She opened her phone and swiped
through the pictures until she found what she
was looking for. It was an old picture of five Ruby
Girls from their first album.

"Why are there five? I thought there were
only four Ruby Girls?" I asked.

"Good catch, Danny. But look a little closer,"
Vicky said.

Lin leaned in closer to the picture. "No way. Is that really her?"

"Who?" I asked.

"Your mom," Lin said, then looked into Vicky's eyes. "Your mom was an original Ruby Girl?"

"In all her sparkling glory," Vicky said. I don't think I'd ever seen her look so proud. "But I'll tell you about that later. Right now, we need to get to the parade."

"Not without me, you don't."

We looked back toward the sewing machine and saw our gray-haired seamstress dressed like a punk-rock superhero.

"Kathleen. You look awesome," Lin said.

"Do you think Penny will be surprised to see me like this? Because there is no way I'm letting you go back to the Microterium without me," she said.

"Now you're talking," I said.

"And now we're walking," Vicky said as we headed out of the costume truck.

# CHAPTER 12
## EVERYONE LOVES A PARADE

"This might be the craziest thing we've tried yet," I said as we walked boldly out of the costume truck and made our way to the line of parade floats.

"And that includes trying to hug a spinosaurus in a swamp," Vicky said as she waved to the crowd.

"Great costume!" someone dressed like an overstuffed tomato yelled as we passed.

"Thanks!" Lin said with a wave. "But you have to admit, walking out in the open with three Microsaurs is pretty crazy," she said, turning her attention to Vicky.

"We're not walking out in the open, Lin. We're riding," Vicky said. "And don't worry. Riding dinosaurs in a parade is something the Ruby Girls would totally do. Nobody will suspect a thing."

As proof, the other parade attendees shouted

to us as we rode by. "Wow, where did you get those robotic superhero dinosaurs?" "Where can I get one of those?" "Can anyone ride those or is it just you?"

"See. They have no idea," Vicky said.

"The only thing that will give us away is that they don't smell like robots," Kathleen said, and for the first time I noticed that Bruno really did smell like a dinosaur. I couldn't believe I'd spent the entire summer with the Microsaurs and hadn't ever thought that they smelled like anything, but the costume creator was right. They smelled just like dinosaurs.

We had made it to the front of the line of parade floats. Vicky jumped down from behind me, sliding off Bruno's wide rump. She ran ahead. The float was magnificent. Stars the size of sofa cushions rose up out of the float on glitter-covered beams. There were laser lights pointed at a disco ball that seemed to spin in midair, shooting tiny rainbows everywhere, and there were five platforms that spun around slowly, and I was sure Vicky and the four Ruby Girls were going to be standing on those, waving to the crowd soon.

A loud voice boomed out of a bullhorn, and I turned to see a man dressed in a red tuxedo and top hat trying to get our attention.

"All right, everyone. The parade will be starting as soon as our special guests arrive. Our Grand Marshal, Victoria Van-Varbles, is here now, so be alert, people. We're going to be starting soon."

"Where is this parade taking us?" I asked.

"Through the festival, then down Main Street. After that, it turns and makes a loop around the park, and ends back here," Kathleen explained.

"Well, follow us, then. We'll be peeling off before we get to the park and heading toward the Microterium," I said. Kathleen gave me a thumbs-up sign, then scratched the top of Pizza's head as she rode on his back. The playful T. rex looked like he was loving every second of it.

"Sounds like a plan," she said.

The sound of a helicopter whirred from above, and the crowd of parade people turned at once and looked. They started to cheer and holler as the helicopter began to lower toward us.

"You guys ready to meet the Ruby Girls?" Vicky asked.

"Um, we kind of can't leave the Microsaurs out here alone," I said.

"Don't worry. They're coming to us," Vicky said.

The side door of the helicopter slid open, and four women hung

out and waved. The crowd went wild, and I
gasped as they jumped out of the chopper.
For a second I thought they'd lost their minds.
The Ruby Girls slid down on long ropes
and gracefully descended to their spinning
platforms on the float.

"That was AMAZING!" Vicky yelled, and I had to agree. It was one heck of an entrance.

Vicky took her spot on the float, and she motioned for the Ruby Girls to gather around. She pointed to us and we waved. The Ruby Girls waved, too, then they motioned for us to come over.

"I guess that's our cue," I said to Lin, but she had already nudged Cornelia forward.

Bruno and I joined in, followed by Pizza and the costume mistress.

"Danny, Lin, this is Shina, Hover-Star, Myracle, and Dash," Vicky said as she introduced us to the

Ruby Girls. We waved, a little too starstruck to say anything.

"And girls, these are my best friends, Danny and Lin, and their amazing robotic pets, Bruno, Pizza, and Cornelia," she said with a wink.

"Great to meet you guys, and your robots are beautiful," the tallest one, Shina, said.

"Lin said you're going to escort us in the parade. It's nice to have you along," Myracle said.

"And if you know the words, sing along," Hover-Star said as music started pumping from a large speaker hidden inside the float.

"Oh, we don't know the words at all," Lin said. "But we'll fake them."

Dash gave Lin a wink and a nod. "My kind of girl," she said, and Lin blushed.

"All right. Let's get this parade moving," the man with the bullhorn said, then waved us on.

We followed the color guard, three men

dressed in their army uniforms, holding the flag and walking the straightest line I'd ever seen. The Ruby Girls and Vicky sang songs to the crowd and Kathleen, Lin, and I faked the words as we rode real-life dinosaurs right down the middle of the street. Not a single person suspected a thing, but boy, did they cheer at how amazing our "robotic pets" were.

We were halfway through the parade when I felt my phone buzzing in my pocket. I pulled it out and saw Professor Penrod was trying to start a video call. I swiped the screen and tried my best to hear what he had to say.

"Danny, your hair looks magnificent," he said, looking shocked to see me with a bright blue Mohawk.

"Wait till you see this." I swung the camera around, showing him his sister, Kathleen, and Pizza.

"Oh my goodness. Those costumes are amazing. I can't wait to see them in person," he said.

"Can't wait to show them to you," I said. "I hope you have some good news for me."

"I do. It's why I called. I found the issue

with the Expand-O-Shrink-O-Portal.
Everything is working perfectly now,
and we're ready to have you back.
Where are you?"

"We're about to leave this parade
and meet you in the Microterium," I
said.

"Excellent. We'll see you soon," the
professor said, then hung up. I clicked
the Invisible Communicator in my ear
and connected with Lin and Vicky.

"Okay. It's time to make our escape.
When we get to the corner, we turn the
Microsaurs to the right and head to the
Microterium," I said.

"Sounds good to me," Lin said.

"Vicky. Thanks so much for all your help today.
We couldn't have done it without you," I said.

She stopped singing for a while, turned off
her microphone, and responded. "You don't need

to thank me. I'm an IMPA member. It's my duty," she said with a grin.

"Still. You rocked today," Lin said.

"Oh, I know," Vicky responded in the most Vicky way ever.

I motioned to Kathleen to follow me when we got to the corner. It was kind of hard to push through the crowd of parade watchers, but when you see something the size of Bruno heading your way, not to mention the rows of teeth Pizza and Cornelia can flash, you tend to scooch.

The twins went through first, parting the way, and just before I made it, someone jumped on Bruno with me. It startled me so much I almost fell off.

"Vicky?" I said as she wrapped her arms around my shoulders and held on tight.

"You didn't think you were going to the Microterium without me, did you?"

"I thought you would like to spend time with

your heroes," I said, knowing that the Ruby Girls were the most important thing in Vicky's life.

"Silly. Friends are way better than heroes," she said. "Come on. We're falling behind."

I gave Bruno a nudge, and he stomped after Lin and Kathleen and their galloping T. rexes.

# CHAPTER 13
## BACK TO NORMAL

"Oh my goodness. I haven't laid eyes on this home for more than twenty years," Kathleen said as we entered Professor Penrod's backyard through the hole Bruno had ripped in the fence.

"Twenty years? How long has Penny lived here?" Lin asked.

"This was our uncle Percy's house. We grew up just down the street, but we came and played in this backyard almost every day. I'm sure Penny has told you all about our uncle Percy," she said, leading us through the deep grass.

"Not really, actually," I explained. "We've seen his field guide, and Professor Penrod said that his uncle was a big inspiration. But that's about it."

Kathleen Penrod stopped in her tracks, then turned to look back at us. "I cannot believe my ears. The stories of Perciful Penrod are the most adventure-filled, dangerous, crazy stories I've ever heard. He is one of the most important micro-paleontologists of our time. I'm going to give that brother of mine an earful when I meet him. He should have been sharing his stories with you from the start."

"I can't wait to hear them," Vicky said.

"Me too, but I also can't wait to get these guys back to the Microterium," Lin said.

"Of course. Carry on," Kathleen said, then continued to mumble to herself as we walked to the barn-lab.

I hurried ahead and opened the door. Kathleen went in first and looked around.

"Well, this place hasn't changed one bit," she said.

"Really? I am shocked. I thought for sure this was all new stuff Professor Penrod put together," Lin said.

"On the contrary. This is all Uncle Percy's equipment. I will say that Penny has done an excellent job of preserving the place, though. It is like stepping back into my childhood," she said.

"Well, if you think that is a big step, just wait until you step through the Expand-O-Shrink-O-Portal," I said with a grin.

"I'll turn it on and you push Bruno and the twins in," Lin said.

"That's a great idea. You guys go ahead and shrink, and I'll be right behind you," I said.

I propped the door wide open by leaning a shovel against it, then went back to get the Microsaurs moving. They were tired. It had been

a long day for them, too. Bruno was leaning against the apple tree, munching on sour apples that Cornelia had bashed from the tree earlier in the day. The twins were lying in the grass, enjoying the summer sun.

I heard Kathleen scream, in a happy way, as she shrank. Hearing her voice go from normal to so tiny a bee couldn't hear it made me giggle.

"Come on, you three. It's time to go home," I said. They all looked at me like I was crazy, which wasn't too much of a shock being that I still looked like a punk rocker who had been dunked in a glitter bathtub.

"There are snacks in there," I said, trying to get their attention, but still, nobody budged. Then I had an idea. I took off my backpack and found the jar of emergency peanut butter I always carry around with me. I went to the apple tree and found an old branch that had fallen off so long ago that it was brittle and crispy, Bruno's favorite type. As I slathered the stick, I talked to Bruno.

"I get it, big guy. You want to be big. I mean, that's what your ancestors were like, right? It must be fun to be big enough to smash a Tomato-Mobile." The twins were getting curious.

They stood up and walked over to see what we were doing.

"And you, too," I said. "It's gotta be great to be so big you could scare away a whole crowd of people with one simple growl. Actually, there are times when I wish I could do that for sure."

I finished slathering the stick. Bruno licked his lips and chuffed. I let Pizza lick off the knife as I put the lid back on the jar.

"But even though you might think it's fun for a while to do something new. Something wild and awesome. To be someone else or act like something totally new. In the end, it's always better to be yourself. You guys are not big scary dinosaurs. You're Microsaurs, and that's not just okay, that's downright amazing."

I stood up and put on my backpack, then carried the peanut butter stick toward the open barn door.

"So, what do you say, big guy? Are you ready

to go back to the Microterium? I can't guarantee there will be any bumper cars to smash inside there, but I can tell you two things. One, there is no doubt that behind that Expand-O-Shrink-O-Portal you will be surrounded by friends. And two, when you are surrounded by friends, good things happen," I said.

After flicking the blue switch to turn on Professor Penrod's new and improved invention, I tossed the stick in through the barn. It shrank

in an instant as it flew through the Expand-O-Shrink-O-Portal. Bruno tilted his head and looked at me a bit confused.

"Go on, bud. It's just through there. Adventure AWAITS!" I said. Then I slapped his rump and Bruno charged, leading the way for Pizza and Cornelia and me as we zipped into the Microterium.

# A MESSAGE FROM PENROD

Tap, tap, tap!

"Hello? Are you there? Is that you, fine reader?

"Well, if it is and you're still reading, then I assume that it is. I must admit, it's been nice having you along for the adventure. Danny, Lin, and Vicky have been through quite a lot, and knowing that you were always there cheering them along has made all the difference. In many ways, it would have been impossible without you.

"But now it's your turn. Yes, yours. It's time for you to continue the Microsaur adventures. Go forth and discover! Study and be curious. Look in the most unexpected of places. Make yourself a fine grass suit if you think that will help. Because they are out there, and they need our help.

"And of course, like any good scientist, keep a record of your adventures. Write them down. Share them with friends. Sharing is the best way to help them now. Get their stories out there. And perhaps I'll have a few of my own to share as well.

"So . . . I guess this is it. Time for me to say

good-bye, but have no fear. As long as there is adventure out there to be found, I'll be around.

"Until then, remember, adventure awaits!"

# FACTS ABOUT TRICERATOPS

- Professor Penrod was right to be surprised in *Follow That Tiny-Dactyl* when Danny discovered that the color red was what was driving Bruno 2 crazy, because scientists have discovered that most dinosaurs, including triceratops, were actually color-blind.

- Triceratops horns changed shape as they grew older. Young triceratops, like Bruno, had short,

stubby horns, but the
adult triceratops had
long, sharp horns
they used to protect
themselves from
aggressive carnivores.

- Triceratops never had
  a chance to eat peanut
  butter, but they probably would have
  loved it. They were big plant eaters, also known
  as herbivores, and their sharp beak and powerful
  crushing molars helped them eat everything from
  flower blossoms to roots and nuts they dug up
  with their big, beaklike noses.

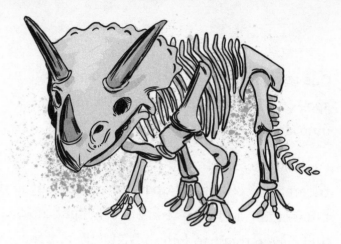

- The first fossil of a triceratops was discovered in Denver, Colorado, in 1887. However, it wasn't until John Bell Hatcher found a nearly complete skull in Wyoming in 1889 that the dinosaur was given its name.

- The name *triceratops* actually means "three-horned-face" in Greek. Makes perfect sense.

- Some triceratops may have had as many as eight hundred teeth! And you thought it took a long time to floss.

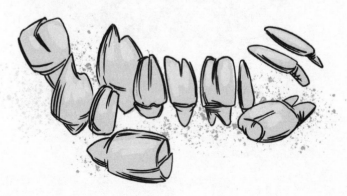

- One thing Bruno 2 taught us that was actually spot-on: The triceratops was not a very fast dinosaur.

- Fossils today show us that a fully mature triceratops could grow up to thirty feet long and ten feet tall, and weighed between eight thousand and eleven thousand pounds. If a triceratops stood on a basketball court, it could touch the three-point line with its tail and lick the backboard with its tongue at the same time.

# ACKNOWLEDGMENTS

I can't believe this happened so fast. It seems like only yesterday I was rummaging through Hilmer Peterson's old barn, mystified by all his dusty tools, the bolts, screws, and nails in all those tiny jars, and his stacks of *National Geographic* magazines. It wasn't long ago that I went "adventuring" with my cousin Brent, who had come to visit from Idaho, with backpacks full of snacks, walking sticks we found along the way, and a wary eye for the rattlesnakes that often crossed the same paths we walked. And the memories of finishing reading my first "big book" on my own, *Nanook of the North* by Robert Flaherty, and wanting to write stories of my own are as fresh in my mind today as they were four decades ago.

Telling stories and drawing pictures about the adventures in my mind has been a lifelong pursuit. And sharing them with the world has been nothing short of a dream come true.

It's impossible to imagine this all happening without the help of a large extended family. My agent, Gemma Cooper. My editor, Holly West. The amazing team at Feiwel and Friends, including Jean Feiwel, Liz Dresner, Emily Settle, and so many more.

My immediate family has been there every step of the way. My sons, Davis and Tanner, helped coloring in some of the pages found in these books. One daughter, Annie, helped name the Microsaurs and tell silly jokes, and my other daughter, Malorie, performed the voices of Danny, Lin, and Professor Penrod in the audiobook. But I can't begin to express how much time and support my wife, Jodi, gave along the way. She read every horrible rough draft, listened to me brainstorm a bazillion bad (and a few good) ideas, and gave me encouragement when I thought I simply couldn't do it. To these five bright stars in my life, I can't thank you enough.

And of course, to you, dear reader and members of the IMPA. Your enthusiasm for reading and sharing your stories has been the driving force behind this series. Without you, this simply wouldn't have happened. Thank you from the bottom of my heart.

And so it draws to a close, and I'm left quoting old you-know-who. Professor Penrod. Ready to say it with me? Here we go.

Adventure awaits!

**DUSTIN HANSEN**, author of *Game On! Video Game History from Pong and Pac-Man to Mario, Minecraft, and More* and the Microsaurs series, was raised in rural Utah. After studying art at Snow College, he began working in the video game industry, where he has been following his passions of art and writing for more than twenty years. Dustin can often be found hiking with his family in the same canyons he grew up in, with a sketchbook in his pocket and a well-stocked backpack over his shoulders.

Thank you for reading this **FEIWEL AND FRIENDS** book.

The friends who made

# MICROSAURS

## TINY-TRICERA TROUBLES

possible are:

**JEAN FEIWEL**, Publisher

**LIZ SZABLA**, Associate Publisher

**RICH DEAS**, Senior Creative Director

**HOLLY WEST**, Senior Editor

**ANNA ROBERTO**, Senior Editor

**KAT BRZOZOWSKI**, Senior Editor

**VAL OTAROD**, Associate Editor

**ALEXEI ESIKOFF**, Senior Managing Editor

**RAYMOND ERNESTO COLÓN**, Senior Production Manager

**ANNA POON**, Assistant Editor

**EMILY SETTLE**, Associate Editor

**ERIN SIU**, Editorial Assistant

**LIZ DRESNER**, Associate Art Director

**STARR BAER**, Senior Production Editor

Follow us on Facebook or visit us online at mackids.com.

**OUR BOOKS ARE FRIENDS FOR LIFE.**